THE
CARNIVALE
INTERVIEWS

TESTIMONIES OF THE SUPERNATURAL

FIRST EDITION

TEXT, ART AND DESIGN BY JCHOOPER

INDEX

INTRODUCTION

Ladies and gentlemen, welcome to the age after the carnage of the Great War. It's the 1920s and times are changing. It's a time of renewal, hope, and a new perspective on life. The lessons learned were costly, and now we pursue a discovery to live more fully, with purpose, and newfound identity.

Allow me to introduce myself: my name is Pete Hooper, and I am a freelance writer who travels the country finding exceptional people and documenting their stories. I am fluent in a few languages and sell my stories for a living to newspapers and magazines. During the summer I was passing through Croyde, a small town in located at Devonshire, southwest England, when I first got the news of a traveling circus, the Carnivale. Given the nature of my work, I simply couldn't resist to attend. So, I did, and to my surprise, became absolutely astonished at what I found. I saw the first few performances and was hooked, so decided to stay for the whole show.

I discovered this magnificent group, composed of all women, who run the circus. Their bond of sisterhood is clearly visible. At first, I thought of them as extravagant freaks or fanatic gypsies: but as often is the case, discovered there is much more beneath the surface. Their way of life is non-conventional; the amazing performances, strange outfits, and spirit of independence, speaks of a group of unique rebels, united by a common value system, their faith. That was a surprise. They are deep in their faith even though their lives are not traditional at all.

This collection of interviews is about the personal stories of the main performers of the Carnivale. The stories and testimonies are as surreal and exciting as their performances. Although their stories are supernatural, I found them sincere and believable: it really serves no practical purpose to inflate or exaggerate. This is how it went: I approached their leader, and she agreed for me to interview them, with a few conditions. These interviews were not to obstruct their duties. I could also ask details about their personal lives, and they would share as they saw fit, but the center theme was to be their testimonies of faith. The conversation had to be about their unique stories. I agreed to the requests and started the next day.

Being very religious, bearing false witness is not in their core, so it is obvious they deeply believe their experiences and events to be true. Furthermore, they promised to be honest with me, and I was to report their stories accurately and without censorship. As a seasoned reporter, I wonder if a certain amount of spice was added here or there. But

hey, after all, they are performers and there is no harm in adding flavor to a good story, as long as it sticks to the truth.

The best way to document these stories is to present transcripts of the interviews, word for word. I am confident you will find awe and delight in the stories they shared. All these are inspiring personal accounts of overcoming challenges, as well as their supernatural and spiritual experiences, that they witnessed firsthand. Some of these stories are as fascinating and bizarre as their livelihood.

Well, without further delay, here are the interviews for your delight. Don't forget to visit the Carnivale when they make it to your local town. You won't be asking for your money back. Guaranteed! •

LA MARIPOSA

FLYING HEARTS

When I requested permission to do these interviews, the performers voted, and after some deliberation, I was allowed to proceed. The only performer that wasn't thrilled to participate was La Mariposa. She said it was annoying. The group then suggested I should start with her, and if I survived, then I could proceed with the others. She rolled her eyes, but then smiled.

La Mariposa, is a tall, muscular, blue-eyed blonde that rides a motorcycle. Her performance includes stunts where her mastery of the machine is in display. Her bold outfit and strange makeup, along with the loud engine, crafts an aggressive and intimidating first impression. Just about when the show is about to start, the musicians play drums in a rhythmic pattern that builds up, and suddenly a few barrels are lit on fire, making for a quite dramatic entrance. After the initial deafening roar, Mariposa proceeds to ride her motorcycle, taking off in a hurry.

Without giving away too much, I can say the stunts are hair-raising: flying through the air, neatly displaying a bond between human and machine. The audience screamed, clapped, and cheered through the performance. She closed with a flirty gesture and a kiss; the crowd loved the show. We met a few minutes afterwards for the interview. Here is the full transcript:

Pete: Hello! Thank you for remembering our interview. I must say, that was quite the show; very impressive. I guess you must be a little tired after your performance.

Mariposa: Thank you, Pete. Just because you are a non-threatening ordinary looking male, it doesn't mean you don't deserve respect, nor that I would be scatter-brained as to forget the appointment.

Pete: Well, thanks... I guess.

Mariposa: I am curious; is Pete short for Peter or is that the actual name your mother gave you?

Pete: It's just Pete. Allow me to start by asking a few things about your past. Is that ok with you?

Mariposa: Ugh. Ok.

Pete: I can tell you have an accent. Where were you born?

Mariposa: I was born in Spain.

My parents moved to England to try to escape the Great Influenza epidemic. Ironically, they got sick and passed away. There was no way to locate my extended family so that is how I ended being sent to live with the nuns. I learned English at the orphanage during my youth.

Pete: Yes, we all grew up got scared of the Spanish flu. I am glad we survived it. Too bad for those who didn't. I am very sorry about your parents. Nobody can blame them for trying to protect you.

Mariposa: Thinking back, they should have stayed in Spain. Who knows, maybe they wouldn't have died if they weren't so afraid of it, but that is the past. I know they meant well. However, there was a time I felt partially responsible for their death. I struggled with that growing up.

Pete: I guess that was a burden for you: imagining all the scenarios.

Mariposa: Yes, it was hard getting rid of the victim mentality.

Pete: I guess the nuns helped somewhat.

Mariposa: They did, in a big way. They were very loving to me and helped with my anger and resentment issues. But you know, fear was the tricky one. For the longest time I felt alone in the world. But you know, that is not the case anymore. I realized God always sends us a helper; there is always someone with us. I want to tell you about a nun: sister Martha. She was always kind and loving to me, even when I wasn't. To be transparent, I confess I was ugly sometimes. She taught me to see life in a different light: it is not what you get, but what you give, that matters most. She truly lived that way, and she changed me, for the best.

Pete: So, the tough, mean personality is just an act to go with your show?

Mariposa: Ha ha ha. Well, maybe. I must say that I enjoy being a little scary. I prefer to take initiative and lead, because the truth is, I am still a little scared to put another person in charge of my destiny. This is why I am not married and ready to follow a man. I know I am attractive because I get plenty of male attention, but at this point I prefer my freedom. I guess my sisters feel somewhat the same way I do.

Pete: This might sound a little harsh, but you are not a society of man-haters, are you?

Mariposa: Nope. Some of us have had lovers, even husbands, but we don't stick around anywhere very long for anything to get serious.

It's more of a platonic type of love. We travel a lot, and we stay only a few nights on each town. All of us have a bond of sisterhood; this is our family. We take care of each other, and we work together for the common good. Selfishness, narcissism, laziness, helplessness, you won't find that here.

Pete: So, you have had some love interests. Tell me: is it hard sometimes? Don't you want a man to take care of you?

Mariposa: I do want a family one day, but I have not met the man of my dreams. Sorry to disappoint, but it is not you, if that is what you are implying.

Pete: Ha! Love that. Nicely put. You like being unreachable. Don't you?

Mariposa: I am just playing with you. Hey, they warned you about me, right? Men like the chase, the challenge. Nobody values the easy girls.

Pete: Agree. Most people prefer a challenge.

Mariposa: The same is true for my show. Listen, you always pay a price to win; you must make sacrifices to become valuable. I don't get an audience by just looking pretty and doing boring stuff; it is my skill and my craft what brings people to see the show. I have to put the work in. There is a lot of practice involved. The performance you just witnessed took several months to perfect. You put your energy where it is going to be most rewarding. I don't want to waste my days daydreaming of the man I met last week, who lives too far away to visit, that I will probably never see again. That is a luxury I don't have right now. Who knows, maybe in the future, but not now. I am still young and want to see the world. When I meet my prince charming, I will know it.

Pete: You are a realist. So how did you get into motorcycles?

Mariposa: My father had a few motorcycles. He taught me to ride at an early age. I inherited it when he passed. The nuns did not allow me to use it until I was a little older. It took some convincing, but when they saw I could ride, they relaxed a bit. As I got older and join the Carnivale, I upgraded, and have done so since then. I have a talent for it. I also like working on the machines, the maintenance and customization to my preferences.

Pete: I am sure the nuns were scared to let a little girl ride. It's atypical and against instincts.

Mariposa: Yes. It is uncommon for little girls to ride. I remember begging them to let me, only to say that I was going to get injured or killed. But I knew that was not my destiny; I knew that I would not die in an accident.

Pete: How can you be so sure?

Mariposa: We all have the Holy Spirit in us. We just have to listen. He guides and protects us. This does not mean that we should be tempting God. On the contrary, we should never do that. We need to be fearful and respectful, and if we are, He will direct our lives. He will give us mental strength in the hour of testing. We cannot allow others to dictate our destiny. Do you know how many times I have heard people say to me what I should do or not do? They have said I would never succeed, that I would get hurt, that I should do something else. They said it is not good to live the way I do. To all of them, I give them this.

Pete: The infamous middle finger.

Mariposa: The Spirit of God gives us power, love and self-discipline. The people that love me support me. If I really want something, I must work for it. It is up to me to make it happen. I will not put my destiny in the hands of another person. The world is not fair and will eat you if you let it.

Pete: I agree with what you say. It is true. People that don't want you to succeed will hinder you and your dreams. They said the same thing about me. They said I would starve as a writer. It's not easy, but we all must make our fight. Is this your testimony? How did you know God was by your side supporting your ideas and not just you being stubborn? How can you tell?

Mariposa: I do not hold the absolute truth. God is the only one. Knowing this, the best way to know if what you are doing lines up with God's plan for your life is to study His everlasting word, and to listen to the Holy Spirit talking to you. We all know when something is wrong. We hear that voice inside our head saying don't do it. Like the fear of jumping from a great height or when stealing. We all know it's wrong. Perhaps a child doesn't know, but once we become older, we know darn well. The opposite is true when we do the right thing. We can see the fruits of our labor. If we are doing something right, we get a reward. We always reap the harvest of our works.

Pete: Do you equate success with money?

Mariposa: Sometimes. Money is a tool, a resource. It should never be the goal because when we die, we cannot take it with us. On the other hand, if God blessed you with ample resources, you should use those to help others, and further the kingdom; not just for the purpose to accumulate more of it. That is greed and it's pointless. I believe that those who have been trusted with more have more responsibility that those who don't have as much. I find it unattractive when men try to impress me with their shit. I have received fancy gifts, but I am not a whore for rent. I do like nice things, but I am not selling my integrity. What matters to me is a man's personality, who they are as an individual, their value system, their manhood. If they like me as a person, for who I am, for what I have overcome, for what I can do, then I let them in. If they are just chasing after me because I am hot, forget it. They are just a boy chasing a new toy. I have learned greedy people tend to be slimy and neurotic, and I stay clear.

Pete: Certainly, you must agree love comes into the heart through the eyes, most of the time.

Mariposa: Yes, I know it sounds harsh, but it doesn't take long to figure out who the idiots are. I do have standards and will not settle for less than I deserve. I have broken a few hearts, and it is much less pain to break them than to have mine broken. I am not easy; I have worth.

Pete: Do you pray about this?

Mariposa: Absolutely. You can pray about anything. You can pray for wisdom, for clarity, and God will give it to you. I prayed, and often do, for wisdom and guidance. God never disappoints. Never. God is love. He loves everyone. Even you, little Pete.

Pete: Tell me about when that person broke your heart. What did you learn?

Mariposa: Yeah, that player. I met this man when I was 16 and fell in love, hard, but he turned out to be controlling and would manipulate my feelings. I was naive and didn't know better. It was hard to break that relationship. In a way I am grateful because I learned a lot, and now, I am much more selective. Love can blind us, and this is why I am very careful to whom I give my interest. I observe them like a hawk; I often test them. I approach romance with patience.

Pete: Any advice for younger girls?

Mariposa: Yeah. You can overcome anything by faith and love. God can give strength and restore a broken heart. Give all your love to God and you will never be disappointed.

Pete: Fun ride. Thank you, Mariposa. •

LAS GEMELAS BOWIE

NEVER ALONE

My second interview is actually with two performers, the Bowie twins. Two for two. Ha ha. Joking aside, their performance was quite scary and thrilling. It ended well and nobody got hurt. Someone getting seriously hurt was a present possibility. Throwing sharp knives around, towards people, juggling them, etc. It was quite entertaining. I cannot explain why, in a certain dark way, I was hoping to see someone getting hurt. Of course I am not a sadist, but why else would I be watching a show about knifes? Ah, I have the answer: because the people throwing the knives are two beautiful identical twins.

The Bowie twins, Pepper and Rachel, are visually indistinguishable one from another. Their outfit and makeup reminds me of a funeral; all black. Their skin is pale white, and contrasts sharply with their dark brown eyes. The show was very entertaining, and it was a combination of humor, thrill, and awe. They are very good at what they do. It was especially interesting to me, because during the show I was volunteered to be tied up to a large spinning target, where they threw dagger after dagger at me. That is correct. I didn't really want the extra attention, but I guess they wanted me to experience the show fully, by being part of it. I closed my eyes a few times, but I am still in one piece and without harm. Here is the interview:

Pete: Hello ladies. Even though we just met a little while ago, I feel that we have a bond due to surviving some perils together.

Pepper: Yes! I had fun too!

Rachel: Come on, Pete. You didn't even bleed a little.

Pete: And I am very glad for that. I like to stay whole and healthy.

Pepper: You are whole, but you could probably use some exercise.

Pete: Hey!

Pepper: Ha ha ha. Just kidding with you. We think you are fun.

Pete: Really? What makes you think that.

Rachel: You might have not realized it, but you were smiling while we were throwing knives at you.

Pete: I was scared.

Pepper: Yes, but you didn't cry. That earned you points.

Pete: Thank you. Enough about me; let's talk about you. How did you end up working at a circus as knife-wielding performers?

Rachel: Our father was the town butcher. Ever since we were little, we were around sharp knives and meat that needed processing. He taught us how to properly care for knives, and to distinguish different metals and blades.

Pepper: That is true, but as you can imagine, we didn't want to follow that line of work. How many female butchers do you know?

Pete: Agreed. When did you both know you wanted to perform?

Pepper: We used to carry knives with us since we can remember even as little girls. We learned early on that knives have the characteristic of attracting attention, and we love it.

Rachel: True. There is something very satisfying about performing and hearing a crowd clap for you.

Pete: Is it all about the show?

Rachel: Yes, it's an honest way to earn a living and certainly beats cutting animals in tiny pieces. Also, a girl loves to dress up, and we get to do that every night we perform.

Pete: Fair enough. Were you recruited by the Carnivale?

Rachel: We attended one of the shows as young girls, and we ran away. We never looked back.

Pete: Wow! You left your family just like that?

Pepper: That is not correct, Petey. Can I call you that?

Pete: Sure.

Pepper: My sister and I became orphans, and we didn't like it. The nuns were fine, but they didn't want us to have knives. They were concerned and in order to prevent accidents, they took them away. That was our identity, and that didn't sit well with us. We were criticized and ostracized. We were ridiculed and they just didn't get us.

Pete: You left the orphanage, joined the Carnivale, and started performing, is that right?

Rachel: You got it. You must fight for your rights and make your own destiny. If they don't like who you are, it's time to leave.

Pete: For some people, it takes a lifetime to reach that level of conviction. Most people prefer to compromise.

Pepper: Look, Petey, we are not psychos, and we know it. We like knives, know all about them and are really good at throwing them. Some people like guns, we have one of those in the crew. You will like her too.

Pete: I am not judging you! Please forgive me if I gave that impression. I am just trying to understand how you can be so temperate and casual about this unusual skill.

Rachel: A sharp knife can cut its wielder as well. You need to be cool-minded. You cannot hesitate or loose concentration. Fear is not helpful, but you must respect the tool. It is not a toy. We have used knives to protect ourselves too. Remember we were orphans?

Pete: Oh wow! Tell me about that.

Rachel: There have been times where we had to pull out a knife to prevent and assault. A weapon is a good equalizer. In one instance, this weirdo followed by two large dogs was coming my way over a bridge. When we were in close proximity, his dog got very close to me. I asked him to put a leash on his dogs.

Suddenly, the man became rude. I guess he didn't like me telling him what to do. I explained I have been bitten before and asked again to control his animals. The argument escalated and he became aggressive. He threatened to hurt me and started moving towards me. I was obviously in danger, so I quickly pulled a knife. I made sure he saw it. When he saw I was ready to use it to defend myself, his appetite for violence quickly faded. Like a bucket of cold water was poured over his head, he stepped back and walked away. The best part is nobody got hurt, all thanks to a knife, and my willingness to use it. If he would have seen me hesitate, someone would have gotten hurt, and it was not going to be me. Let me be clear, I don't advocate violence in any way, but our world is full of crazy people.

Pete: I am sorry you had to experience that. You certainly are very courageous.

Rachel: Thank you. I was not going to give him a chance to hurt me. I have always have a knife on me, ever since I was a kid.

Pepper: I had a similar experience as well. We had already joined the Carnivale and while at this town we were passing through, this man kept staring at me in a weird way.

When the show was over, I noticed he followed me to my quarters. Once there, he tried to engage with me. At the beginning he was friendly, but then he said something meant to shock me. He said not to be scared, but he had a knife and was not going to use it if I gave him what he wanted.

Pete: Oh, no.

Pepper: At that moment, I reversed the roles. I pulled out my knife and told him he better leave, or I was going to use it on him. I was very convincing, because the man backed off and raised his hands telling me to calm down. My reaction escalated, as I started yelling at him, and at that point he run away. He probably thought I was totally nuts.

Pete: No way! That was epic!

Pepper: Yes, that is called righteous anger. He deserved every little bit of it.

Rachel: Agree! You did good, little sister. You are so brave.

Pete: I hope he learned his lesson. You are both so courageous! It takes valor to do what you did.

Pepper: Petey, we are no victims; neither from evil ones, nor from

our circumstances. We face our challenges head on, with resolution and hope of a good outcome.

Rachel: Yes. Sometimes the threats we face are not as clear as these.

Pete: What other threats are you referring to?

Rachel: Let me explain. There are good people in this world, that try to help you. We are convinced God sends you angels to help you. But many times, evil is in disguise and hard to spot. The sneak attacks are the toughest ones. Evil can try to influence you through temptation, or coercion. It can be through social rejection or pressure. They will try to make you sin, to abandon your heart and succumb to pressure. What matters is to stay true to your values and morals.

Pete: You said God will send you angels. Can you elaborate on why you believe that?

Rachel: Sure. I have had encounters with angels. I cannot say if angels are people God sends at the precise moment you need help, or if they are truly angelic beings. But I would like to share with you a special story that happened to both of us. You can then decide for yourself.

Pete: Yes, please. Tell me about it.

Rachel: Pepper, would you like to tell him this story?

Pepper: Sure. My sister and I were at the orphanage, riding an old and rusty bicycle. The chain kept coming off. It was a nuisance, but that's all we had. We were trying to make it work. On one occasion, the chain came off and I was trying to get it back in gear. Of course, I was using my fingers to do the work. Suddenly my fingers got caught very badly in between the gear and the chain. It was very painful. They were stuck and I remember crying.

Rachel: When that happened, I tried frantically to free her fingers, but with every attempt it was getting worse. I was terrified she was going to lose them. We were on the back of the orphanage, and nobody could hear our cries for help. I went down again on my knees again. Then, out of nowhere, a man appeared. He asked us what the problem was, and he proceeded to free Pepper's fingers.

Pepper: Yes, I remember him as tall, strong and gentle man. When my fingers were fee, I realized they were not badly hurt, just a few scratches. I hugged my sister and cried of joy. Then we realized the stranger was gone, in a blink of the eyes. It was impossible because there was no way he could have

walked away so quickly. In addition, there were no men allowed at the orphanage, and we were inside the property, behind a tall wall meant to protect us.

Pete: Unbelievable.

Rachel: It is true. The experience changed us for life. It cemented our belief that suffering is for a purpose that we may not comprehend, and we are never truly alone. All we must do is have faith, do our part, and we will persevere. If it is too much, God will send help.

Pete: That is beautiful. Thank you for sharing. •

DIANA LA CAZADORA
LIGHT AND DARKNESS

When I first walked into Diana's private tent for the interview, I noticed a handful of handsome medals hanging from the wall, cast in various languages. A few minutes later there she was. A true toxophilite, Diana is a soft-spoken woman; mysterious, rather tiny in size, with tan skin and long black hair which contrasts with her piercing light grey eyes. Her show was different than what I expected. She was working the crowd in a rather elegant and poised performance. Her showmanship was her skill, which was almost scary. It was like witnessing the training of an assassin or a ninja; professional and very effective.

She has no equal when it comes to her ability with the bow, displaying total mastery and dexterity that is beyond awe. Arrows are obedient to her thoughts, and it seems they can change direction mid-flight. For example, during her performance she was able to strike multiple small moving targets, that were thrown in the air all at once, with a rapid-fire volley. She executed trick shots that were hard to believe. At one point she released multiple arrows with one pull, and they all successfully hit their intended targets. To witness her skill during the show is well worth the admission ticket. It was so inspiring it made me want to become an archer myself. Here is the transcript of the interview:

Pete: Nice to meet you, Diana. I must say I enjoyed your act.

Diana: Certainly.

Pete: I noticed the medals over there. I assume you won them in important competitions.

Diana: Correct. Most are mine. I have collected a few shiny things.

Pete: You don't brag about your achievements: that's the mark of a champion.

Diana: Thank you.

Pete: Let's begin with your heritage. You don't appear to be northern European, are you? Where did you grow up?

Diana: My mother was Native American, of the Cherokee tribe, to be precise. She fell in love with my father, a Scottish hunter, who happened to be traveling through America in search for adventure. Somehow, he convinced my mother to come to the old world and marry him. Tragically, my mother passed during my childhood. When I was 9, my father went to fight in the great war, and went on to live with my grandmother. A few years later my father was killed in France. My grandmother got sick and passed away. With no other family around I was assigned to live at an orphanage in Scotland.

Pete: That is very tragic. I am sorry. Let's move on, if that it's ok with you. When did you become interested in archery?

Diana: My father is the one who taught me how to use the bow. I have very fond memories of him teaching me. He preferred the long bow, but obviously it was too large for me to use as a child; I couldn't even pull it. He crafted a smaller hunting bow sized to fit me, and by the age 7, I was proficient enough to hunt small game, such as squirrels and rabbits.

Pete: It must have been a very important part of his life for him to want to transmit that skill to you.

Diana: My father was so adept with it that he was allowed to use it during combat, apparently quite effectively. A few of the medals you saw over there, were awarded to him. Upon his death, they were delivered to me, along with his long bow. It's the one hanging over there, over that wall.

Pete: Oh, wow. It's a little scary to know that bow over there was used in the war. Going back to when you were a child, how did you manage to keep that weapon in the orphanage?

Diana: Yes. Thinking back, I have no idea why they would let me keep it. I would use it unsupervised. Maybe it is because they didn't know I could actually use it. Maybe they had other problems to take care of.

Pete: You were practicing in secret.

Diana: Yes. As I grew older, my skill grew as well. I have always been a loner. Obviously, there was no one was around most of the time. The nuns would focus on the squeaky wheels, if you understand what I am saying. I was quiet and kept out of trouble. That awarded me much freedom.

Pete: Stealthy.

Diana: Yes, I don't like people controlling me; I am free and I do as I please.

Pete: Did the guardians at the orphanage eventually find out?

Diana: No. I left in good terms. I was sometimes annoyed that other kids got all the attention, but I never wanted to trade who I was for them.

Pete: The nuns failed at taming you. Do you think you have become your father's image?

Diana: Well, my father had a reputation. He was definitively a good hunter; he made a living doing so. However, I do not kill for a living. I refuse to follow that path. I am the product of love, of two different cultures, it is in my blood. I obviously grew up here, but I learned enough from my mother's culture as well. I am trying to honor the best of both.

Pete: You have that spirit running through your veins.

Diana: I will be eternally thankful to the nuns as well. My father was a Christian, but they are the ones who really taught me about God. They made me study the Bible and that was very good for my spirit, it helped me.

Pete: Tell me about that. Can you elaborate?

Diana: They taught me how to channel anger into something positive, something for good. When my father died, I was broken, angry. I had no one. The pain was so strong I became self-centered and couldn't see past my own suffering. I know I would have not been able to get past those negative thoughts without a personal relationship with Jesus. Only by His word, His Grace I was saved. He gave me perspective, I overcame fear, depression, anger, and resentment. He gave me a better way: love, kindness, courage, fortitude. God always comes first for me. He is my rock, my most important relationship. I have learned to experience His love in my daily life, and I am able to find Him in the world around me. It is like learning to read tracks in the dirt, to really understand what those signs mean. It's all there, but you just must learn how to look. Sometimes you must wait, and sometimes you must go and find. And when you find it, the truth reveals beautifully. This knowledge equipped me with hope and peace, to see life in a different way. It also gave me hope for the future, when I will reunite with my family in heaven, face to face, and embrace them.

Pete: How did you find God? Was it during your catechism?

Diana: Yes. The defining moment for me was my first communion. I still remember it so clearly. I suddenly felt hot all over. I started to sweat when the Holy Spirit touched my soul. This warm feeling took over me. In that instant, I knew I was loved and cared for, at peace, protected. It is hard to explain, but I became fully aware at that moment. It was beautiful.

Pete: Sounds like the fire spoken of in the Bible.

Diana: I have learned that God has a plan for every one of us. Perhaps this is why my parents were taken away from me, so I could develop a different relationship with God, other than the one they had. I don't know. Sometimes is hard to make sense of things. But I know there must be a reason for the suffering. I refuse to believe it's for no good reason or purpose.

Pete: I agree. Tell me the story of how you end up here, at the Carnivale, becoming a performer at a traveling circus?

Diana: I often wondered why God put me here. I joined the Carnivale pretty young. I saw the caravan in transit one day, when I was in the woods. I was very curious about what I saw, so tracked them down to their camp at the outskirts of the nearby town, which was about two miles from the orphanage. I went in to explore; I saw what was going on and that same night I knew I had to be part of it. I fled the orphanage. I felt they were weird like me, in a familiar way. I knew I belonged and never looked back. That was ten years ago. During these years, I realized that it was all God's plan. I would have never seen the caravan if I wasn't out there, practicing with my bow.

Pete: Seems like it was a perfect coincidence.

Diana: I disagree, I don't believe in coincidences. Everything happens by God's design. He has already planned things for all of us before we are born. We must live life and then, when you look back, everything makes perfect sense. It's a perfect plan. We are created for a purpose and that is very reassuring. I know we are to face challenges to test our faith, and that produces perseverance. It has given me strength, a sense of purpose and worth.

Pete: Have you had any other experience, that could validate your ideas? One that could serve as confirmation that it is not all in your head. Perhaps a revelation that cannot be denied?

Diana: Yes, I have had a few, but one comes to mind. It happened shortly after I arrived at the orphanage, I was still young, maybe eight years old. It was a cold night, in the middle of winter. I was sharing a bed with another girl. We were poor and everything had to be shared. From our bedroom we could hear wolves howling in the distance. I was a little scared to hear their howls, blending in with the sound of the wind coming in through the window frames. We started praying intensely, with the innocence only children can. We prayed for God to spare the sheep, for them not to be eaten by the wolves. We asked Him to protect them. Even though we had experienced so much pain growing up, our hearts were still pure, we were innocent. I guess we were praying like angels do. Suddenly, the dark room started to light up! A bright light appeared in the room. A candle could never be that bright. It made the room as bright as day. We were not scared: it felt peaceful, familiar, comforting, and beautiful. It lasted for a few moments only. Then, just as sudden as it came, it was gone. We were in darkness again. I asked my friend if she saw it and said yes! Somehow, I we knew God had heard our prayers and sent and angel as a sign. The howling stopped and we didn't hear it for the rest of the night. The sheep were safe.

Pete: That is a beautiful story! Did you tell someone?

Diana: We did. The nuns questioned if we were making it up. After all, we were little girls, you know. However, that experience taught me that there is a God that is very real, always present, protecting us, who cares about what we do and what we say.

Pete: It is true that adults sometimes can be skeptical. If only we had the eyes of a child, to see things in a different light.

Diana: I don't mean to be rude, but we will have to stop here. I have things to attend to. Nice talking to you, Pete.

Pete: I understand. Nice to meet you, and thank you for your time. •

LA SALAMANDRA

PURIFIED GOLD

Today has been a hot day. It has cooled a little now that it's dark, and the Carnivale shows are starting. This is my second night performing interviews and I am excited to interview La Salamandra. She is a fire juggler, the queen of kerosene. I saw her show on my first night here, and because her act is later during the night, we agreed to have the interview earlier tonight. She is a woman with red hair and pale skin. She has green eyes and a thin complexion.

La Salamandra is certainly an entertainer. She starts her routine by performing a rhythmic dance much like a traditional ballerina, to the beat of drums that change pace as she moves around the stage. During the dance, she displays her incredible flexibility. At a moment, her toes touch the back of her head; her spine seems double-jointed.

There are a lot of dangerous flaming things that are thrown into the air. If you have ever witnessed a professional juggler, It certainly requires lots of skill and dexterity, but to add fire to the equation really elevates the performance. As with the other performers, I will not publish details of the act with the exception that towards the end of her performance, she lights herself on fire! Yes, I know it sounds really crazy, but she does. Obviously, it is all part of the act, but oh boy, what a shocker! Here is the interview:

Pete: Hello Salamandra. Thank you for allowing me to interview you.

Salamandra: You are welcome.

Pete: Your show was enthralling; I really enjoyed it. You move with such grace!

Salamandra: Thank you. I am glad you enjoyed it.

Pete: I have seen shows of jugglers before, but I have never seen one like yours. Also, I have never seen someone on fire. That was quite scary and impressive. How were you able to do so?

Salamandra: It's a secret. I could tell you but then I would have to kill you.

Pete: Ha! Don't tell me, then. Let's start with the name; why do you go by La Salamandra?

Salamandra: The word salamander comes from Greek origin meaning fire lizard. Also, salamanders are nocturnal, and can regenerate better than most creatures. That fits me well. I like the concept of being put through fire to be purified, like gold, just to emerge better of better quality, better than I was before.

Pete: Interesting! How did you get started as a performer?

Salamandra: My performance career started with beauty pageants, when I was a teen. I took lots of dance lessons, many hours practicing how to walk and have a good posture, etc. I became a total prat. I won a few regional titles. It didn't come easy. In the beginning I was shy but after some time I realized I could do it.

Pete: I understand pageants can be quite harsh. I have covered a few as a reporter.

Salamandra: Yes. It was hard. But experiences I had growing up helped greatly. When I was young, I was too focused on getting approval from others and it became an unhealthy struggle. Once I overcame that, pageants were actually fun. I had more confidence that my competition. It's very competitive but it didn't consume me. I felt like it was a chance to earn some money and open doors for success, that's it. I would never measure myself constantly against others like I did when I was younger. I didn't affect me in a negative way. Judging is up to others to decide. I know who I am.

Pete: How you were able to see it that way? To see it as an outsider, rather than being pulled under by the current.

Salamandra: I joined pageants not to seek attention and approval from others. I have rather focused on being better person; I much rather working on myself and all that is underneath the surface. It wasn't always that way. I was super thin when I was a teenager, and I hated my own reflection. It was a real struggle.

Pete: I can relate to that. I was super skinny growing up as well.

Salamandra: I would like to expand on that experience. Is that, ok?

Pete: Yes, please.

Salamandra: I want to be clear that what I am about to share can be sad, and is very personal, but my experience can give hope to someone who is going through a hard situation. My goal is to help someone who struggles with self-esteem. Perhaps this has been the result of constant berating and ridicule from others. People can be very cruel sometimes. Usually, the ones that are the meanest are very insecure themselves. Others are just jerks, or just plain evil.

Pete: You are correct.

Salamandra: When we are young, we tend to believe everything that peers tell us. We can easily be led through a dark path of being self-critical. This can be magnified by our insecurities. Especially when we are in our teen years, everything can be so scary. Our bodies are changing, and our hormones are wild. We get pimples everywhere, and we think we are getting uglier by the minute, with no way out.

Pete: I am having flashbacks.

Salamandra: Going back to when I was a teenager, I disliked my body so much that I didn't value myself at all; I felt worthless. One day I saw my thin body, and devastated by the image in the mirror, I broke it in a million pieces. I felt my body was all there was to me; and I didn't like it. I avoided looking at my reflection wherever I went.

Pete: How did you get to such a dark place? You are certainly a beautiful and confident woman today. You perform in front of crowds a very perilous act.

Salamandra: My physical appearance was lacking, but it was not only my body the issue; my friends started making fun of me, they would call me names, sing hurtful songs and I really felt isolated. Then the bullying started. Some of them were very cruel. They would openly say things like: "how can she stand on those toothpicks", or "her skin is so white because she drinks too much milk". They would make fun of the color of my hair. These comments were devastating to me, as a young girl. There was so much pressure to be beautiful, to look a certain way, to have certain features. I didn't have any of those, the physical attributes that would make me acceptable to them. I became depressed and introverted. There was no joy in living. Every day was sad and empty. The emotional abuse was coming from everywhere and I didn't have a support group, a best friend or anything like that. I couldn't find peace, and like a snowball, the longer it kept going, the bigger and heavier it got.

Pete: I am sorry.

Salamandra: The enemy is sneaky, and it attacks when you are most vulnerable. Voices start to whisper in your ear, until you are drowned in sadness. The voices, combined with the constant abuse and bulling, pushed me to honestly believe I was worthless. I felt it was a mistake I was born. Just like a defective pot, I had to be broken and thrown away. One night I went as far as to put a knife on my wrist.

Pete: Oh no! Poor girl! You must have felt there was no other way.

Salamandra: I saw no other way. I thought it would be better if I was dead. I was crying and felt hopeless. Who could possibly ever love me? A despicable bag of bones. I was convinced I was a total waste, a failed experiment. As I started to put pressure on that knife, I suddenly heard a voice in my head. It was not an audible voice, but I clearly heard it. It was a very strange thought, in the sense that I would have never had it on my own. I am convinced it came from somewhere else. Somewhere outside my brain. It was a message that opened my eyes, it changed my way of thinking immediately.

Pete: What was the message?

Salamandra: The message was: why are you giving all those people so much power? Why do you care about what they have to say about you? You don't owe them anything. You should send all their opinions to the trash and get yourself a new life. Get rid of them; push them out of your life. Do your own thing. You do not need to believe them; who are they anyway? They are not you, and your identity is not who they say it is. You are not who they say you are. Don't believe that. Don't throw yourself away, never.

Pete: Amazing! I am going to cry.

Salamandra: I immediately felt warm. It stopped me on my tracks. I put that knife away and I smiled. I knew that was correct! I have listened to fools long enough! I know that message was from God, because I was not in the state of mind to think that way. A message with such wisdom and hope. It was incredibly liberating. Ever since that day, I have never put my sense of self-worth in the hands, or mouth, of another person. I am free. I do not need them.

Pete: That is very inspiring and true. Thank you. How do you suggest someone can be more fulfilled, and have a better sense of worth about themselves?

Salamandra: I try to love others more, even those who have been ugly to me. This is really hard, but forgiveness is key. Also, I try to be fruitful in my spirit, by trying to be more joyful, kind and gentle, patient, more faithful. To conclude, I would like to bring attention to the fact that our bodies are just that, bodies. They will change over time. They are not eternal. What we really need to concentrate on is our inner beauty as I just described. Yes, it's hard when our bodies are sick or don't behave like we would like them to, but remember true beauty does not come from the outside, but from the inside. We have unfading beauty that is treasured by God, our creator. We are His masterpiece. He made us exactly as He wanted us to be, for a specific purpose only He knows. We are not accidents, we are unique.

Pete: Thank you for sharing such a beautiful story of overcoming. I am sure it will help someone.

Salamandra: Pete, when you interview someone that seems lonely and sad, please encourage them. Lend them your ears and don't offer solutions, just listen. Offer some empathy. You may just save a life.

Pete: Will do. Thank you for the interview. •

28

AGLAIA LA TRAPECISTA

NOT OF THIS WORLD

The trapeze is possibly one of the most traditional acts in a circus. I have seen a few in my life. Somehow, the trapeze is both respected and feared. The thrill comes from the fear of falling. I am afraid of heights, so to watch Aglaia perform gave me that. That is something I could never do, no matter how much I tried.

Aglaia is a redhead, and her pale skin and green eyes scream Scotland. What is surprising is her natural strength. She has clearly been trained in gymnastics, as evident in her floor routine, prior climbing the tall stairs to the top of the carp, where she flies through the air to the amazement of the crowd. It is a beautiful but scary performance. I would be terrified just to climb up that high! Music and dance join in a celebration of rhythm and acrobatics.

When I interviewed her, she came across as sad but firm; her gaze was gentle but wise. You could tell she has seen things that most of us never do. She puzzled me because for someone who is so attuned with her body, she seemed to be elsewhere, in a distant world. Here is the interview:

Pete: You have nerves of steel!

Aglaia: Thank you.

Pete: I want to start by telling you that I suffer of acrophobia, so I could never do what you do. I take my hat off to you. You must train a lot. You are very strong.

Aglaia: I do train quite a bit.

Pete: How did you get started? When did you decide to make this your craft?

Aglaia: I have always had good balance, and have been very physical. It all started when I was a child, always doing crazy things on the playground and elsewhere. When I started to grow up, my friends kept telling me to do this or that to amuse them. My hobby became my profession when I joined the Carnivale.

Pete: That is lucky. Most of us cannot claim that. I am sure you are aware of this. Congratulations!

Aglaia: Yes, I am very happy. I like what I do. We all have our gift. I guess yours is writing.

Pete: That is what they tell me. Let's move on. During the interviews I have made, I have been learning that all the performers have some beautiful supernatural stories to share. I was hoping you would be willing to share yours.

Aglaia: Are you a believer, Pete?

Pete: I am a Christian.

Aglaia: Good. Are you warm or lukewarm?

Pete: I am not following. I go to church. What do you mean?

Aglaia: The reason I ask is the stories I am about to share deal with supernatural things that have happened to me. The stories have a good ending, but can be hard to believe, and a little scary. I just want to make sure you are comfortable talking about such things, like ghosts and spirits.

Pete: You are scaring me a little.

Aglaia: Do you believe in things you cannot see? Do you believe in the spiritual world?

Pete: My salvation is in Jesus Christ. I cannot see Him, but I can see His works and how He transforms His Church. I believe in the Holy Spirit. Yes, I believe.

Aglaia: The testimony I am about to share is about some experiences where I had to learn to trust, keep my balance, and blindly trust in my Lord, Jesus. Some of them might seem weird, but I assure you they are true.

Pete: You have my full attention. Is there a specific one you would like to start with?

Aglaia: Hmm. Yes, I think I would like to tell you in the order they happened. Ever since I was very young, I have felt that evil spirits have wanted to control me, as if I was some treasure or cash price. They have attacked me from many angles. When I was younger, they would torment me on my sleep. They would give me horrendous nightmares. When I would close my eyes and started to fall asleep, I would fall through a hole, deep into the ground. It was very dark. I remember feeling scared and not wanting to go there. What made these dreams exceptional is the content. None of friends ever had this magnitude of dreams. Now that I am much older, I understand that they were supernatural attacks by evil spirits.

Pete: How can you be sure of that?

Aglaia: The dreams were always the same. They were very systematic, like indoctrination. They always started the same way. At the beginning I was dragged into this dark hole in the ground. It was the precursor indicating I was about to enter a nightmare, and I couldn't stop myself from being sucked into it. At the end of those nightmares, I would always wake up right before I was about to die. The funny thing is, I was never afraid of death while I was awake. I was not a happy child, and I could care less about this world. I was always scared when the night came. I guess I was afraid to die in those unholy places, surrounded by evil spirits. The reason why I state these were in fact, the whispers of demons, is because when you have contact with the supernatural, something about the barrier that separates what we can see and not, what we know and don't, gets thinner.

Pete: Can you please elaborate?

Aglaia: Sure. The first dream that comes to mind is the one where I was performing an exorcism. I was 10 years old at the time. It was many years later, when I actually read about how an exorcism is performed, I realized I had experienced one in that dream. How can a child know that? I could have never known of such terrors on my own. It has no explanation.

Pete: That defies logic.

Aglaia: Exactly. There is no way a 10-year-old girl can know those things.

Pete: Did they subside?

Aglaia: Yes. I remember the turning point was right at the beginning of a nightmare, when I was about to be sucked into the hole in the sand pit. I refused. I said no! I remember clearly stating I was not going in there anymore. Then, it suddenly stopped! It worked, but then the spirits changed tactics, they became more aggressive. The place I grew up was haunted. I couldn't wait to get out of there, but I had nowhere to go.

Pete: How did you know the place was haunted?

Aglaia: Because there were supernatural experiences that went beyond dreams. I have a gift: I can feel spirits, I know when they are around, sometimes even see them. That house was full of evil nasty demons, I am sure of that.

Pete: Can you mention something specific that happened in that house that revealed those spirits?

Aglaia: The house had a staircase. I could not use the staircase normally. I would feel pressure on my chest when going up, or feeling like there was somebody right behind me when going down. I had to put my back against the wall and walk upstairs that way. I would choose to run when going downstairs, it helped.

Pete: How do you know it was not your imagination?

Aglaia: One night I was awoken by a nightmare and ran to my mother's room. I never did that before, but that time I was very scared; I felt the presence of evil very strongly. I knocked on her door, but she told me to go back to bed. When I turned around, I saw it! I looked like a girl, my age, with long black hair, about my size. She had a horrible stare and was smiling at me. Her eyes were solid black. She started walking towards me. I frantically banged on the door as she approached me. She was closing in and right stretched her arms to grab me. Just right before she touched me, I closed my eyes. The door finally opened, and my mother was upset. She scolded me for waking her up in the middle of the night. I didn't care about the punishment to come tomorrow; at least I was safe.

Pete: Did you tell your mother about what you had experienced?

Aglaia: Of course not. She would have thought I was crazy or making things up.

Pete: Did that occur again?

Aglaia: No. I received my first communion a few weeks later, and the spirits stopped bothering me. A sense of peace came over me. I didn't understand it completely at that time, but now I know it was the Holy Spirit shielding me. God saved me, He sealed me and claimed me as His own. With that came the gift of protection. I could still feel them in that place until we moved out, but they would keep their distance. Most spirits are confined to a specific place.

Pete: Have the attacks stopped since then?

Aglaia: Mostly, but I recall another strong attack years later. I woke up in the morning and couldn't move, literally. An evil spirit was holding me down, like sitting on top of me. I was fully awake, but I couldn't speak. I couldn't see it, but I could feel it. It was heavy and the weight was suffocating. Then I took a last breath and was unable to continue breathing. I remember hearing an angel in my head telling me to fight, to resist. Somehow, I knew that if I could move any part of my body, even if it was a finger,

I would break the attack. It was all about will. I knew my life was as stake. I saw my own body from above, I was floating above the bed, and saw this nasty spirit sitting on my chest. I refused to surrender and as soon as I moved my thumb the spirit screamed and fled. I felt joy, because I learned I could fight them and be victorious. Now I had the spiritual strength to do it. I still have a few bad dreams sometimes, like everyone else, but those experiences are a thing of the past, thank God!

Pete: Wait, I thought once you are baptized and give your life to Jesus you cannot be attacked.

Aglaia: I wish that was true. The truth is a believer you cannot be possessed by an evil spirit. However, evil spirits can always tempt or hinder you. They can oppress. They can try to scare you too. That is always an option. Through the years I have felt a few spirits trying to attack me, I am still a prize to them, but they cannot have me. I can resist them and deny them. I am stronger now because I have given myself completely to God. I belong to my Lord, my shepherd. The blood of Jesus protects me. The evil ones have lost their edge against me; I am now much better equipped to fight them.

Pete: A scripture comes to mind. The book of Ephesians 2:8 reads: For by grace are ye saved through faith; and that not of yourselves: it is the gift of God.

Aglaia: Yes! You know your Bible!

Pete: I try. Why do you think God has allowed these experiences in your life?

Aglaia: When I look back, I realize the enemy has revealed himself to me. Consequently, he has proven the existence of the spiritual world to me. Evidence of their existence demands a creator, a superior being. That is why the devil is always hiding, trying to make us believe he isn't real. Well, his cover is blown. I fully believe in God. I can fight spirits, through the strength that God grants me.

Pete: Thank you for sharing your powerful testimony.

Aglaia: Peace •

OLIVIA LA TATUADA
HEALING ART

Olivia's show is certainly artistic. The show starts by her drawing beautiful pictures as she reads poetry. The poetry takes several interesting turns, and talks about love, betrayal and reconciliation. She is covered in tattoos. Even though she starts the show fully dressed, towards the end most of them are all gone, and all the tattoos are revealed.

The show is not sexual or manky, but I am told it's a common occurrence during the show to have men catcalling. The performance I witnessed got a little wild towards the end. I noticed a woman getting into an argument with her significant other, as she attempted to cover his eyes, and then smacked him. Surely, he said something dumb. Olivia doesn't mind the extra attention and stays cool throughout.

Olivia has an abundant collection of drawings in her tent. She is talented with graphite and oil. Some are self-portraits, while others are portraits of random people. Apart from the show, she also sells sketches of circus attendants, for a modest fee. All the artwork on display is available for purchase as well. Here is the interview:

Pete: Nice to meet you, Olivia.

Olivia: Nice to meet you as well.

Pete: I can see both talent and technique in your work. Have you always been good at art?

Olivia: Yes. I have always had that gift. I was lucky to have great instruction as well, which helped me become a master of my own style; to discover my own art.

Pete: I am always impressed at people that can draw; I cannot draw to save my life! By looking around, I can tell you have a favorite subject matter for your art.

Olivia: Yes! The human form. I believe it is God's masterpiece. The most beautiful thing in creation must be us; built to the image of our Creator.

Pete: What specifically attracts you about people?

Olivia: Well, it's not so much their appearance, but their soul, and how it reflects in their expression. To me, the human form, especially the face, the eyes, are a window to the soul. You can see an individual's life speak as reflections on their faces. Some eyes are sad, while some are cheerful and mischievous. Some are painful, some are comforting and familiar. All that can be articulated without saying a word. People can say anything or act tough, but they cannot hide the history displayed on their eyes. Some eyes are flat and desolate, while some are dense and voluptuous. Some are full of life while some are dying. Some people try to hide their insecurities, while others use their eyes to enhance their beauty.

Pete: I have heard that an artist tries to find beauty in everything.

Olivia: True. There is beauty in brokenness too. We just have to find it. Some people spend their lives chasing money, dreams, sex, power, or others. I prefer to chase beauty. I try to find it in everyone.

Pete: Do you think there is therapy in what you do, your art?

Olivia: Absolutely. I thrive on finding beauty. It is my favorite thing to do. I don't like selling my drawings, but a girl has to make a living. I do keep some favorites around. We travel a lot, so we are limited on what we carry.

Pete: What do you feel when you create art?

Olivia: I feel everything is right. Art is not simply copying something; art is an interpretation, what you feel, what it means to you. The first thing I do is set up an environment where I can create. No loud noises, no distractions. That is why I paint without looking at the audience: to stay in the zone. I immerse myself in the canvas. It starts with a feeling. For example, first I ask the person a few questions, like who is this painting for. Then I start to explore and to pour into the canvas all those feelings; what those eyes are telling me.
I add my interpretation as I see fit. Some come easier that others, but sometimes I see something that I didn't quite get at first. It is like opening their story and putting it on the linen or paper. I don't claim to understand everything about everyone; I like to observe. It is just about that specific moment. Art is meant to communicate. An image can mean something different to a different audience Some people relate to a feeling they experienced themselves when looking at a portrait of somebody else. Perhaps a memory or something else.

Pete: That makes sense. When did you first realize you had a special talent, a gift?

Olivia: I was very young, perhaps at the age of seven. I made a drawing of a clown I saw at a show. My mother kept telling me it was very special, and she wanted me to make another one for a friend of hers. Soon after that, people started to notice, and it never stopped. I used art to escape my circumstances because I didn't like my reality. I found refuge in art, it would keep me busy and I loved it. I had control over what was happening on that piece of paper, and there was so much to learn.

Pete: Can you share what were you trying to escape?

Olivia: Family issues. My parents used to fight a lot in front of me. They eventually got divorced. They remarried but unfortunately the stepparents didn't care much for me. With all the chaos around me, I was somewhat neglected. I never went hungry, but the adults in my life didn't pay attention to me. I don't remember ever getting help with schoolwork, or them attending important milestones in my life. They were consumed with their own problems. The worst was the physical and mental abuse I endured from the stepfather. He was a real winner, not.

Pete: I am sorry. Some parents shouldn't be allowed to be. They cause more harm than good.

Olivia: Thank you. The stepbrothers were encouraged to be mean and would destroy my creations. I was isolated at home and school, both emotionally and socially. Those experiences pushed me inwards, and consequently, I learned a lot about myself. In retrospect, that pushed me to grow artistically.

Pete: Was school a shelter for you?

Olivia: No. It was terrible as well. I would get hurt. I got beat up constantly and had several broken bones through the years.

Pete: Ugh. You were bullied. Not fun. Tell me how you prevailed.

Olivia: I was very thin when I was a young teen. I was so thin that people would ridicule me. I felt gammy and unworthy. They didn't know me as a person, so my body was my identity to them. My self-esteem was zero. Sometimes, even art was not enough. You cannot sit down to draw when your coccyx is broken, or when you are so angry you just want to hurt someone, because you are hurting so much. I was so depressed I contemplated suicide. But one night, during a dream, I heard an angel who told me I was God's masterful creation, and He cared about me. He told me there were many great things planned for my future. This was a major turning point. God loved me at my darkest time! I will never forget that.

Pete: Beautiful! That message couldn't come soon enough for you, I suspect.

Olivia: Correct; it took a little while to sink in, but then I started to bloom, and everything changed. Boys started to take interest in me. Those girls who were mean to me didn't grow up as attractive as I did, and suddenly wanted me as a friend, so they could also get some attention from boys. I despised them for that.

Pete: I mean no disrespect, but you turned out all right.

Olivia: I did. I am very comfortable in my skin.

Pete: I can tell. Talking about that... tell me about your tattoos. What's the story behind them? How it came to be that your body is a canvas? Have you painted your own body?

Olivia: Of course, you silly.

Pete: Some might consider tattoos a barmy decision. I know Christians are not supposed to mark their skin. How do reconcile that?

Olivia: Ha! They are not permanent. I use a special water-resistant ink of my own design that will stay on my skin for a little while. I like transforming myself into a work of art. On the religious aspect, it is not an act of disrespect or rebellion, but rather an expression of art on a different canvas. I would never ink myself permanently. In addition, I would surely get bored with a specific drawing that is permanent, and there would be no way to erase it; I have the need to be constantly creating new work.

Pete: I have another challenging question for you, if you allow me. Why do you get undressed in front of an audience of strangers? Isn't that immoral?

Olivia: Is it immoral to see a statue or a nude painting in a museum?

Pete: I guess not.

Olivia: Here is my logic. I am going to be very honest: I love the attention. I am beautiful right now and I don't mind showing my beauty. It is part of my show, and I earn a living. I don't sell myself. I think it's ok. I was made fun of when I was growing up for being too ugly. Now people admire me. It makes me happy.

Pete: Do you believe beauty is age-related?

Olivia: Yes and no. We all agree there are primes in life. For a man it usually happens during his 30s or 40s. A woman can be at their prime much younger, from late teens to 30s. There are exceptions to this, of course. I love drawing children and elders as well. It's not about what is considered attractive, it's about beauty. Eyes don't age; some people are born with cheerful, beautiful eyes and some are born with ancient eyes. Some of my better paintings are of older people.

Pete: You are lucky to have that gift; some people go through life without doing what they really like for a living.

Olivia: Thank you. I don't care too much about money. My gift is mine, and I do with it the best I can. So far, so good!

Pete: What would you say to someone that is currently isolated and struggling?

Olivia: Always wear a smile. Regardless of your circumstances, it can help a lot. There are very bad people in the world, about one in ten. They are the destroyers, the troublemakers. Avoid those at all costs. On the other hand, there are the good people, also about one in ten. These are the creatives, the builders. Find them and keep them. Lastly there are a lot of insecure people in the world, that is the vast majority, and they can do bad things to hide their insecurities. Both good and bad people influence them. Be one of the good ones. Just remember every good gift is from above, and you are no mistake or accident. God doesn't make mistakes. God made you the way you are for a reason, for His purpose. Be yourself.

Pete: Wise words indeed. Thank you for time and your testimony.

Olivia: Stay beautiful. •

LA VIUDA NEGRA

CURES AND REMEDIES

Meet the brains of the Carnivale: la Viuda Negra. I met her before, and she approved this whole endeavor, but we met briefly. Today I get to talk to her more deeply. She is not the oldest of the group, but there is something about her that exudes leadership. She is obviously well liked and respected and has done a good job at keeping the Carnivale successful.

There was a change in the air as soon as I entered her chambers. I looked around the room while waiting for her to arrive. Delicious aromas and a sense of mystery floated in the air. Even though her quarters are modest, she holds a sizable collection of tiny artifacts and little pots labeled with exotic contents. Some I recognize, like mint and juniper, but others I have not heard of. They mostly contain aromatic substances and leaves, likely used to craft her perfumes and potions.

A few minutes later she arrived. Of elegant walk, she was wearing a black dress and black boots. She is of average height, has black hair and blue eyes. Her makeup heavy and dramatic. She looked at me like a lion studies it its prey. I stood up to greet her as she walked through the room with a polite smile on her face. She sat down, crossed her legs, and tapped the chair closest to her, signaling me to sit there. Here is a transcript of the interview:

Pete: Let me start by thanking you for the opportunity to write about your performers. Interviewing them has been great so far!

Negra: My pleasure. Please go ahead with the interview.

Pete: All right. I understand you are an alchemist. Did you inherit your skills from your family?

Negra: I would not call myself that. I have a few family recipes, but most of the knowledge I acquired through schooling.

Pete: Are you saying there is actual science behind your products?

Negra: I am disappointed, Pete! Did you think all this was all a scam?

Pete: Are you saying your potions really work?

Negra: Yes! I get that a lot. The potions and perfumes I sell do their intended purposes quite well. Through the years I perfected my formulas. You would be surprised what you can learn from traveling and local libraries.

Pete: I mean no disrespect; tell me more of the elixirs you brew.

Negra: I have practical knowledge to heal most common ailments with herbs and plants. Sometimes I act like the town physician, when we travel through tiny towns who do not have a doctor. However, my best sellers are potions that address issues of the heart.

Pete: The heart?

Negra: Yes! You would be surprised how many people are lonely; how many people love someone without being loved in return, how many people are sad and heartbroken.

Pete: And you claim you can cure those things?

Negra: Most of the time. Other times I can only offer relief.

Pete: Please forgive my lack of faith. I am trying to understand. You claim to make love potions that actually work?

Negra: Indeed. It's not bluffing if you can prove it. You see, every person has individual needs.

When someone books a session with me, I do a comprehensive understanding of the situation. Then I figure out a way to help. I am proficient in the art of brewing love potions, among a plethora of other products. I can succeed where physicians fail, where traditional medicine has no power. I have been gifted with the ability to heal not only certain bodily ailments, but also emotional struggles. I have remedies for sadness, anxiety, anger, just to name a few. I offer something to everyone who comes to my shop. Sometimes the remedy is a path forward, or a change in habits. It really depends on every situation. I have a responsibility to use my gift to help, and not to hurt. I refuse to use it for nefarious purposes. Some of them elixirs are very powerful and dangerous, while others are quite harmless.

Pete: I see. Let's take this one for example. It's labeled "Sweet Surrender". What does it do?

Negra: Ah. Here, darling, drink some of it in this cup. This sweet elixir will first make you feel calm and at ease, but by tomorrow your heart will be mine. I will become the air in your lungs. You will feel physical pain when I am not around you. The effect will not be permanent and will fizzle out, but for a few days you will certainly become my boy toy.

Pete: I'll pass on that one.

Negra: Ha ha ha. I am kidding. That is not what it does, you silly.

Pete: You got me there. What does it really do?

Negra: Sweet Surrender is used to help people who suffer from anxiety. It helps them relax at night. It has a combination of herbs that relax the muscles and quiets the mind. Should only be taken before bedtime, as it will make you drowsy.

Pete: Ah. I see. That makes sense. I feel like a fool. Maybe I am too literal; don't mean to be insensitive. I have misjudged you.

Negra: No worries. I know you are not a prat; you are assertive with your questions. This is why I allowed you to interview my whole crew. I like your boldness and transparency. You are professional.

Pete: Thank you. The last thing I want to do is offend you. Tell me about this other one.

Negra: Hmm. Broken heart. This one I use on different situations. Actually, I used this brew quite frequently during the months following after I lost my husband. It helped me cope.

Pete: You were married! Is that where your artistic name, the Black Widow, comes from?

Negra: That is the case. I was married a few years ago, before I joined the Carnivale. I really loved him. His death was tragic.

Pete: I am sorry for your loss. You must have married very young.

Negra: I was very young. We all face tragedy in our lives. May he rest in peace. If chemistry can help with a particular situation, let's use it. But like I said, it's not all about chemistry. I take the time to talk to the person and understand what is really going on. For example, last week a man came to me asking for a potion to make this girl fall in love with him. You really need to have a sense of humor sometimes.

Pete: The audacity of that man! What did you do in that situation?

Negra: I am a creature of love and believe his intentions were good, but obviously that was the wrong way to go about it; to drug a person is unethical, immoral and illegal. He was just young and stupid. So, I gave him the perfect potion for the situation. I chose Pure Passion. It is basically sugarcane with water. I told him to drink that before he talks to the girl again. I am sure it's unable to hurt anyone with it. It was very expensive as well; I was trying to make a dent on his funds so he doesn't go around finding other options, once he figures out it didn't work out.

Pete: Ha! Perfect! You have a sense of humor.

Negra: I do have very high standards, and my customers are pleased. But like I said, not all is solved by the physical. Some problems require counseling and a little help from the spiritual world.

Pete: Agree. Tell me more.

Negra: I have other gifts, and one of them is the gift of insight. More times than not, I know things about people with just a quick glance, such as their personality, struggles, their trustworthiness, their occupation, let's call it their soul type. That allows me to help them better. I am also good at reading non-verbal language, body language. Most of the time, the body mirrors what is being said. If they don't match, then they are probably being dishonest, afraid, embarrassed, or not disclosing everything. When that happens, it requires further probing.

Pete: How can you possibly know things like their struggles or occupation by just looking at them?

Negra: It is a gift that I cannot explain. I just know by looking at them. It is supernatural.

Pete: Do you use this gift when selecting your crew members?

Negra: Absolutely.

Pete: You are a detective and a therapist. How do you approach issues that require more than a tea?

Negra: Our mind is like a garden. Sometimes bad weeds start to choke the flowers. We need to pull those, so the good thoughts can grow and produce fruit. The weeds I am talking about are almost always the same: lust, avarice, gluttony, sloth, envy, anger or pride. Once you pinpoint the source issue, you can plan a road to recovery. There are instances when I don't sell a potion; it's just my counseling services. I am young, like you said, but I also believe some of us have younger souls, while others have been gifted with more wisdom. Everyone has a gift, and we thrive by using our God-given talents, whether it is our charms, abilities, intelligence or beauty, to name a few. I like to help bring relief to people, to a world full of lonely and misunderstood hearts.

Pete: Your audience is much bigger than I initially thought.

Negra: Yes, almost everyone is looking for a window to escape pain and suffering. Everyone is looking for hope; the ability to see the light. When they have a spiritual issue, I always point them to pray, to get closer to God. You would be surprised how many people don't do that. They believe they are unworthy, that they need a priest or someone else in order to talk to our Heavenly Father.

Pete: How do you approach customers who are atheists or non-believers?

Negra: That is a much trickier situation. I have had conversations at length with atheists. They are so stubborn! It is like they don't want to listen. I think it is because they don't understand. The have a false idea of who God is. They think they are above a person like you and me, at a higher intellectual level. They just don't get it. One of the most common things I have encountered is people blaming God for their misfortunes. There are some people you just can't reason with, and I am left with no option

but to shake the dirt off my boots and leave for the next town, if you understand what I am saying. But to those people who are still young at heart and are willing to listen, it is a beautiful opportunity!

Pete: Why do you do all this? It must be exhausting to hear everyone's problems.

Negra: I find satisfaction in being able to help people. It motivates me. I believe in practicing my faith by serving others. It starts with my crew, and so forth. Life can be abundant if you have the proper ingredients. God gave me gifts to be used for His purpose. We are to make use of these to further His kingdom, while we are in this broken world. We are here to help those less fortunate. God will not forget our works.

Pete: That is inspiring. I think I love you.

Negra: You should. Good night, Pete. •

ADELA LA SOLDADERA

HUNTER AND PREY

Target practice has always been one of my favorite circus attractions, and lucky for me, the Carnivale has one! It brings me fond memories of my own, growing up and trying out my skill. Our father used to bring me and my brothers to the circus, and I happened to be a good shot. I would bring back home a toy after scoring high on the challenge.

The shooting gallery is run by Adela la Soldadera. She is a tall fit woman whose body language and verbal commands are assertive and calculated. She must be in order to avoid accidents. I was surprised to see all the rifles are caliber 22, and not ball bearing, or BBs, as commonly known. The targets are smaller and at a longer distance. It is definitively next level from the standard.

In addition to this, she has posted a sign with an open challenge: "Win cash if you can shoot better than me". It was pricey, but I gave it a try anyway. There were a variety of guns to choose from. I chose the revolver. As you can expect, she is very good. As a matter of fact, she is much better than I am, by far. I lost, but it was worth he shot; no pun intended. Here is the interview:

Pete: Nice to see you again. You could certainly make a living as a safari guide anywhere in the world.

Adela: Ha ha. I could. I just don't like killing animals. This is a much better job.

Pete: How did you become so proficient with firearms?

Adela: It all started when I was a little girl. I was about 7 or 8 years old when my dad taught me how to fire guns. We were living in a rural area where there was no law and we had to learn to defend ourselves. There was some sort of insurrection in that area. He knew that an unarmed child could also be killed by a gun, just like anyone else, so he taught me how to defend myself, because being a victim was not an option.

Pete: That is a little radical.

Adela: Bollocks! It is absolutely true. I am not going down easy.

Pete: Forgive me, but it seems like a bad idea, to teach a little kid how to fire a gun to kill someone else.

Adela: It's not just the use of the gun, it's also the education of when and how to use it. It takes education to know when to pull the trigger and when not to. I know my dad would be very happy today with my skills, if he were alive.

Pete: What happened?

Adela: My parents died of whooping cough, when I was 13, after a trip to Scotland. I was sent to an orphanage where I grew up. When I was old enough I joined the British army and served as an armorer during the Great War.

Pete: I am sorry about your parents. It's so tragic!

Adela: Yes. I was depressed and was looking for death for a very long time. I though joining the war effort would accomplish that sinister goal.

Pete: I am glad that goal didn't work out for you. Now you are such a good shot! I knew you must have had some professional training.

Adela: Yes. That has given me confidence. I am able to defend myself and others.

Pete: I am not surprised to hear that. We all know about the horrors of the war. I am sure you have some war stories you prefer not to talk about. After that experience, how come you are still making a living around guns?

Adela: Guns are not the problem; they are tools. Politicians and rulers are the problem. I dislike bankers and criminals just as much. The world has too many bad people, and idiots that will try to get smart if they can.

Pete: Good point. Criminals prefer easy prey. I had interviewed some nefarious individuals in the past. I can certify that's how they mostly like to operate.

Adela: To be clear, I am not going to make it easy for them to do their dirty deeds. They can find another victim elsewhere. In addition to my range, I am also in charge of security at the Carnivale. We don't have too many issues, but we have had some instances where some force had to be applied.

Pete: Some men find strong women very attractive.

Adela: Are you flirting with me?

Pete: I am just stating a fact.

Adela: Ah. Ok. Just in case: I am not interested in dating. I divorced a two years ago and have no desire to date again.

Pete: That is unfortunate. So much tragedy in your life. Do you want to talk about that?

Adela: Sure. When I was seventeen, I met this man. He was charming, cute, and we were both enlisted. We started talking and he was very direct. He told me he wanted a relationship with me. This man said I was his everything and would never leave me. I believed him. There was something irresistible about him. I had other boyfriends growing up, but never someone that was so into me. It was intoxicating. I fell love and eventually got married. It was not long before he began to change. Perhaps he was like that all along, but I started to notice something different about him. There were some red flags I ignored earlier in the relationship because I was young and in love.

Pete: What red flags?

Adela: He was a non-believer, so our values didn't align quite well. Also, he was a big flirt. It was fine when he was flirting with me, but of course it was not cool to see him flirting with other women. As our marriage progressed, he became controlling, emotionally abusive, and things went downhill from there. I will not want to elaborate on that. All I am going to say is trust was broken, and that was the end.

Pete: So sorry! How have you been able to overcome?

Adela: You know, everything happens for a reason. Many things happen in our lives, but we should not only focus on the negatives. There are also many positives too. Perhaps it's the way you are framing your questions that this conversation seems negative.

Pete: You may be right.

Adela: Life is a balance. We have good and bad together, living in harmony. The pretty and the ugly, like me and you.

Pete: Hey!

Adela: I am just kidding with you, Pete. Lighten up.

Pete: It's all good. It made me laugh, a little.

Adela: For example, guns have served me well. I earn a living on the skills my father taught me. It has also kept me safe from harm. My parents passing has allowed me to be emotionally self-reliant since a young age. I am glad I learned the truth about my ex-husband early on, before I became too old, and wasted many of my best years on that pond scum. There are good things that came from those tragedies. Of course, they were extremely painful, but I am very strong today. I know I can survive things of that magnitude, by the strength God gives me. He has given me health and a sound mind.

Pete: This tells me you have forgiven. You have forgiven so much! Congratulations. Do you believe God cares about everything that happens in your life?

Adela: Absolutely. The Creator of the universe cares about the smallest things concerning my life. He is always present. He watches the decisions we make, and the way we make them. It is not only important to make the right decisions, but where our heart is when we make them.

Pete: I agree. It's not the same to donate because of charity, but out of a sense of guilt or appearances.

Adela: Yes!

Pete: Can you tell me how did you get involved with the Carnivale?

Adela: After the divorce I started traveling. One day I came across the Carnivale, asked if I could join, and they took me in. Negra was very glad I did. I love her.

Pete: I am sure all of them love having you around. You are a natural leader, strong and

confident. Plus, you can provide muscle in case of trouble.

Adela: Thank you. My experiences have made me very objective. I am no longer naive and innocent. I must confess I still struggle with trust when it comes to love. I keep a bullet with my ex-husband's name on it. I do not plan on using, but if he ever comes back trying to find me, I might. That bullet is a reminder of that dark place, a warning, not to give myself away again that openly to another flawed person. Also, my eternal salvation and my relationship with God are more important than revenge, which belongs to the Lord. All the people that wronged me will have to deal with that on judgment day. The only thing left for me is forgiveness. I have forgiven, but I am still healing. As for right now, my family is the Carnivale.

Pete: I am glad you didn't do anything foolish when everything was fresh. You would be in jail, and I would have never met you.

Adela: True. I am a student of the Word of God and there is a simple commandment that most people don't get: "You shall not murder". There is a difference between killing and murder. The condition of your heart and the situation is what makes the difference. If you need to protect yourself or your loved ones, or if you accidentally take a life, like in a train crash, that is not murder. Murder is prohibited and therefore we shall refrain, no matter how justified or entitled we feel. Everyone who sins breaks the law. I do not want to break the law. I love God and the way I show it is by obeying His law.

Pete: I know that forgiving is very important.

Adela: Yes. When you don't forgive, it becomes a poison, your poison. That feeling or bitterness is not hurting the other person, it is hurting you. As far as I know, my ex-husband feels I was at fault, that he did nothing wrong. He is a pitiful poor soul and has no clue. I heard he has remarried and is still drinking heavily. I am glad he is not my problem anymore. I had to forgive him to release myself from that burden. I do not want to carry that bitterness and resentment the rest of my life.

Pete: How do you know your belief system is true? An atheist would just say settle and be done with it. What would you say to another person that does not believe like you do?

Adela: Well, what I have said it's true. I would encourage them to try it out. It has worked for me. It can work for them. If they don't want to receive this wisdom, it's up to them. Have you not heard: "do not throw your pearls to pigs?" Some people are just too stubborn to hear or see otherwise. I would also tell them to give it time. Time is a healer.

Pete: That is good advice.

Adela: I would also tell them to come to the Carnivale and have some fun. Life is too short just to be grinding every day.

Pete: Absolutely! I praise you for overcoming all the challenges you have been dealt with. Thank you for your time. It was fun.

Adela: Of course. And keep practicing; maybe next time you can beat me.

Pete: Not a chance, but thanks. •

NIKA LA PUGILISTA

HEART AND SOUL

In other circuses I have visited, I have seen a Strong Man break chains, and strength challenges involving the audience, but never seen a Strong Woman before. The Carnivale has a ring. Nika walks in with dramatic music and a long overcoat. She then removes it to show her incredibly toned body. She performs a few poses while the men in the audience get a little rowdy. She proceeds to warm up by lifting some heavy weights and such.

The announcer points out to the five of six posters with challenges that the audience can attempt, for a fee. One of those is the push-up challenge: if someone can do more push-ups than Nika, wins cash. Other challenges include sit-ups, arm wrestling, etc. The one that caught my eye was the boxing match: to endure five rounds in the ring against her.

The announcer starts to challenge the audience to get up in the ring with her and engage in the challenges. A few people took the bait, paid their fee and got hammered. During the last challenge, the boxing match, she fooled around for a couple of rounds with a guy, but when he landed a punch on her, she got mad and knocked him out cold. Yes, it sounds barbaric, and it was. But just like the other ladies in the Carnivale, there is more to her than what meets the eye. Underneath that intimidating strength and fierce look, lies an indomitable and cheerful spirit, much stronger than her muscles. Here is the interview:

Pete: Nice to meet you. Thank you for giving me this interview. You are so very fit! I have never seen a woman like you.

Nika: Thank you. It takes discipline. My sisters told me about the interviews you have been making. I have a story for you.

Pete: All right! I am glad you are prepared. Tell me your story.

Nika: I can offer testimony of three different situations where I suffered major attacks on my body; the enemy came after me with the intent to destroy me. God tested me, and also those around me, and helped me overcome supernaturally, no doubt.

Pete: You have my attention. Please tell me all about these attacks.

Nika: The first attack occurred when I was growing up. I was 6 or 7 years old, living in London. When I was a little girl, my parents took me to the doctor, because there was something wrong. I remember being under regular observation. They were observing the way I walked; they were concerned about my feet. The doctors were taking measurements and making molds. I didn't understand, but apparently there was something wrong with my feet, and my legs were getting deformed. The physician's prognosis was dire. My legs were not developing normally. They told my parents I was growing with a malformation, and likely to become a cripple later in life, if no intervention was taken.

Pete: By looking at you, I would have never guessed there was something wrong with your legs.

Nika: My parents refused to give up on me, so they looked for treatments to correct that issue. We saw so many doctors. I recall at least three specialists. I did therapy exercises every morning and night. I had to wear strange orthopedics shoes for years; I would strap them on, right before I fell asleep, and I couldn't move my legs at night because they were bound together. I also had to wear shoe inserts during the day that were painful. It was very difficult. After many

years of perseverance, I was able to overcome and grew up normally afterwards. I remember throwing away in the trash the last shoe inserts in celebration.

Pete: I don't mean to be obtuse, but where is the supernatural aspect of the story?

Nika: It's two-fold. First, there was no family history that could indicate this was genetic. This was clearly a supernatural attack on my body. Second, all the elements required for my cure were gathered because God allowed them to come together at the right time: the unfailing love of my parents, the financial resources required, the expertise of diverse physicians, and my innocence that did not know how to give up. All these people loved me, and this is why I am here today. It not only worked, my legs and feet are perfect now, and I can run short and long distances as I desire.

Pete: You are correct, now that you say so, seems it was a bizarre circumstance, especially since nobody in your family had ever had similar issues. Do you think the hand of God brought everyone together to help you?

Nika: Absolutely. Success happened because God loved me first and surrounded me with people that loved me and wanted to help me: loving parents, resources, and good physicians.

Pete: I am glad it worked out. Tell me about your second attack.

Nika: The second attack came a few years later. I was still a child. We were on a family trip, and we stopped at this restaurant. They had a local specialty, and we all ate, but the food that I ate made me terribly sick. That same night I had a super high fever, which is unusual for food poisoning. There was something terribly wrong. My mother was very worried, and she put me in cold shower in an effort to bring the fever down. This is when I started to see demons. They were staring at me. They were licking their lips, waiting for me to die. They were many of them; they were like men and animal hybrids. They were made from a dark gas and were moving quickly around me. Their eyes were bright red, as if they were lit with a light bulb. They couldn't wait to come and get me; like a vulture roams around the dying prey. I could feel their evil. I was terrified. I started to tell my mother about them, and she said it was just my fever. I got really scared and cried to my mother: "please, don't let them get me, please!". My mother couldn't see them, but she started to pray as she hugged me. I saw the creatures back off. I asked my mom to continue praying, and a

few minutes later, they were gone. My fever broke and I was able to rest and sleep shortly afterwards.

Pete: That is wild! It's scary.

Nika: The enemy wanted to kill me. It was a supernatural attack because nobody just dies overnight because they ate a bad piece of meat; there was something else going on. Also, I didn't take medicine at all, not even afterwards. We didn't go to the doctor for a follow up. I was all well the next morning.

Pete: You said these creatures retreated when your mother prayed over you. Your story gave me goosebumps; look at my arms!

Nika: Demons are looking to kill and destroy, but if you resist them, they will flee. This experience backfired on the enemy, because now I know they exist, they are real. I have proof of the spiritual world. I know they can be fought. They can be defeated. Should we proceed to the third story?

Pete: Yes, please. Go ahead.

Nika: The third attack came much later in life. It happened last year. I was struck with the flu pandemic. I knew it was bad because I felt abnormally weak, under attack. The strange thing is my immune system was not fighting it. I was just getting sicker and sicker as days went by, and I had no fever, nor any symptoms normally associated when fighting a virus. I lost my sense of smell and taste. It was like I was poisoned; like when bitten by a venomous snake. After ten days I was so weak I couldn't walk without a struggle. I tried tons of remedies and rest, but there was no treatment available for my disease. By the second week it got worse, and I got pneumonia. I knew I was dying; I couldn't get out of bed. I made last preparations, and said a very heartfelt and faithful prayer that night. I asked God to please send an angel of healing to help me. I asked God, if it was His will, to send Archangel Raphael to help me that night, because otherwise I felt I was going to be dead by the morning. If God wanted me with Him, I was ready to go.

Pete: You must have felt awful.

Nika: My strength was all gone. That poison or disease had completely drained me. Pneumonia had developed and it was hard to breathe. I fell asleep that night. Then I woke up, at three in the morning. My nightgown was soaking wet. My body had experienced a supernatural healing. It is like the toxin left my body through my pores. God heard my prayer and sent an angel to heal

me! I knew it! I started crying. I was so grateful. I tried everything on my own capacity to get over that, and I was unable. I needed to put my faith completely in God. I did, and it worked! Not by my strength, but through God and his mercy.

Pete: Amazing! I assume you started recovering after that.

Nika: That's right. It was a slow recovery, but I regained all my strength. The experience certainly changed me. I don't see life the same way anymore. So many things are useless, dumb, and not worth of my interest. But the most beautiful thing, is that I know after all these years, God still cares about me. He loves me! He is looking out after me and hears my prayers! I am so amazed and humbled by the fact, that the creator of the universe, of everything that is visible and invisible, lends me His ear and loves me with kindness and patience. My body is just dirt, temporary, but still, it matters to Him.

Pete: Like I said before, I would have never imagined that you were so close to death, just a year ago. How did you recover?

Nika: I am thankful to God for giving me another chance, another round in this fight. You must put the efforts. It pays off. If you put the work, there is always a reward. I am very careful with what I eat. I don't drink. I don't smoke. I am very clean. I work out. I want my body to be as strong as possible, so the attacks of the enemy don't stand a chance at success.

Pete: Your story is inspiring. Do you believe your strength today is somewhat supernatural?

Nika: Some people are naturally stronger than others. You would be surprised. I pray to God every day to strengthen me, so I can do all He wants me to do.

Pete: There is a question still floating in the back of my head. Please humor me. You literally beat people up for a living. Isn't that a bad thing?

Nika: Ha ha ha. I only fight consenting adults. Most people get up there because their inflated egos, have clouded judgment, are drunk, or because pure stupidity, and it is my pleasure to bring them back to reality. I specially enjoy fighting creeps, oh those are my favorites! I feel enjoyment when I see them drooling in the floor after they met my uppercut. Love it.

Pete: That guy you fought earlier was able to punch you. I could tell it made you mad.

Nika: He did get me once. The audacity to hit a girl! He cut my lip and that is why I broke his nose. He deserved it.

Pete: He did. Do you have any advice for people going through difficult situations?

Nika: Whatever it is troubling you, pray. Come to God first, not last, when you have tried everything in your own power to solve your problems. Most battles are spiritual. Become close with God, worship and develop a relationship with Him. He can do anything. He can change you. Also, have a sense of humor. Nothing really matters, life is just a mist. Have fun while you are here. Be strong and learn how to fight back.

Pete: Thank you for your time. I enjoyed your testimony. •

CORA LA SIRENA
UNDER PRESSURE

My next interview is with Cora la Sirena. I have seen her show earlier tonight and it was something bizarre and wonderful. While many circuses have lions or tigers, the Carnivale has a giant fishbowl, where Cora swims, like a mermaid, surrounded by water creatures. She can hold her breath for quite a long time, and she swims around and eventually comes up for another breath.

Her act is unstructured, as observers walk into the space and observe her. They stay for a few minutes, make all kinds of remarks, and leave, allowing the next group of spectators to come in. She is graceful and smooth while she performs a strange but enthralling underwater ballet.

Cora, a ginger with brown eyes, has abnormally dark freckles all over her body. Her marks allow her to blend in with the environment and the other sea creatures. During her performance she was swimming starkers, much to the delight of some male audience members, and the panic of a few mothers with young kids. Oddly enough, she looks like she belongs in there, with the fish. Here is the interview.

Pete: Hello Sirena. Thank you for giving me some of your time.

Cora: You are welcome. Did you enjoy the show?

Pete: Yes, I did. I had a strange thought when I was watching your performance: I was able to see how we, as human beings, have distanced ourselves so much from nature. It is like we are separate from it. You made that gap seem smaller. It gave me the impression all of the creatures and you were one, not apart, but one.

Cora: Wonderful! That is the idea. While it is true that we are very different from the sea creatures, or other animals for that matter, we are still animals. By inserting myself in their environment, as an animal, I can connect to nature in a more intimate and personal way.

Pete: To be honest with you, I have never done that, try to connect to the wild. I can see in your case it works. Is this why you swim without a suit?

Cora: Exactly. It would be weird otherwise. I want the spectators to experience the connection you felt. If I was dressing anything, it would be distracting.

Pete: With all due respect, some would disagree. People don't belong in the ocean, nude.

Cora: Oh well. That is certainly their choice. We are all born that way and leave this world with nothing. Allow me to challenge your perception: Adam and Eve were walking free in the garden of Eden until sin entered their minds. What do you say about that?

Pete: Well, I will have to think about that one. I am not sure everyone needs to be walking around with no garments. You must agree with me that not everyone looks good without clothes, nor should be without proper clothing. I do not envision everyone walking like that at the streets of London.

Cora: Ha ha ha. You are very judgmental. I agree there is a time and place for everything. I do wear clothing when I walk around at the market. Swimming costumes are a different story, they are recent in human history. Consider this, nobody has thought of a newborn as ugly or immoral. It is our culture and the limits it imposes on us that dictate what is appropriate and what is not. I call that sin. Humans are beautiful and marvelous,

an absolute masterpiece, not to be ashamed of. Did you feel embarrassed when you saw me?

Pete: Let's move on. May I ask something about your skin? You have unusual spots all over your body. Are those birthmarks?

Cora: My spots are natural, sort of. When I was a little girl I contracted a strange virus, an uncommon form of chicken pox. That virus left me permanently scarred. They were red at the beginning, and they darkened as I aged. I do love my spots; it is my identity. I like to think my skin looks like that of a cod fish or a seashell. It has brought me closer to the ocean creatures I love so much.

Pete: Yes, they allow you to look like a fish; no offense. Have you always loved the ocean?

Cora: Yes. I have always loved the ocean. My family was from Croyde, a small town in Devon, with not much to do there but the sea. I used to spend most of the day diving, looking for treasures, swimming among all kinds of fish.

Pete: You certainly are very good at swimming.

Cora: Yes, I can easily hold my breath underwater for five minutes. I can go up to ten.

Pete: How did you become part of the Carnivale?

Cora: The Carnivale was traveling and stopped one night at my town. I was immediately smitten by the performers and the acts I witnessed. I begged to join and after some interviews, they adopted me. It is important that we pull our own weight around here. I think my act draws good traffic and therefore I contribute to the success of the Carnivale.

Pete: Our society can be cruel and not very accepting of different things. I am sure you must have had a few sour moments with those spots on your body. How did you handle that chastisement?

Cora: There was a lot of that when I was a kid. Some parents didn't let their children play with me, they were afraid I was infectious or weird. The people I grew up with called me freak and other cruel names. Kids used to make songs about me that would make me cry. Today is a different story. I am very different, and I know I will probably never marry because of this. Who knows. There are still some people that praise me. I love being told I am a mermaid; it is twee to me. I don't mind people staring at me anymore. I do not get negative feedback. I notice some women get upset when they see me

swimming, but it is only the woman that have a male partner with them. Otherwise, they are ok with my act. It is hypocritical, but that is all right. You see, I might be an exhibitionist, but I am celibate. What I do is an expression of art, and my skin is the artwork, and the show I present is an art form. I earn an honest living. Most people really like my act, and that makes me happy. Last week and old lady came over and praised me; she said I was very brave and beautiful and shook my hand. This happens more than you think.

Pete: The fact you turned your problem into an opportunity is inspiring! Good for you.

Cora: The most beautiful fish are not edible, and some are quite dangerous. I identify as this type.

Pete: Ha! Let's go back to something you said: about the old lady praising you. What do you make of that?

Cora: I was able to tell that old woman was very attractive in her youth. She still had that spark in her eyes and her smile. I thought she was sincere. Perhaps my boldness reminded her of some part of her youth. Perhaps she was regretting not being more open in the past? Who knows. Some people live their lives afraid. They are afraid of what others might say, afraid of being

rejected, to become ostracized.
I am over that. I had enough of it,
and I graduated, never to go back.

Pete: How did you make that leap?
From chastisement to confidence.

Cora: It is totally a spiritual battle.
The spirit of oppression is cruel. It
wants you down, quiet, depressed,
pitiful. It wants to reduce you
to nothing; it wants you combat
ineffective. But then something
clicked inside my head. It must have
been the Holy Spirit enlightening
me. I realized the game. All the
people that abused me; who are
they to look down on me? Who are
they to criticize who I am and what
I believe? I am not going to give
them authority over me anymore,
at their deception that they are
better than me. They cannot abuse
me anymore. I will no longer put
up with it. As a matter of fact, I am
better than most. I am beautiful in
my own way; much prettier than
most of them. Even if I am not, I still
have good qualities. I tried to please
them and a peace them, and that
just encouraged them to be crueler.
The truth hit me, and I got off my
knees. I decided to live my life as
I please. I will stand tall and live a
new life. I will live a life pleasing the
only one who truly loves me: God.
He made me the way He intended
me to be. I will do the most of it
with the hand I have been dealt

with. It is my time to shine and
glorify Him by living a life according
to His way, and nobody else's.
I am free! I will never listen to them
anymore; they lost their power
and influence permanently. Those
oppressive spirits can go to hell!
I will shine and be beautiful. I will be
a blessing to those around me.

Pete: Such revelation! Freedom lies
in your heart.

Cora: God called me out of the
darkness into His marvelous light.
My time is now. My mental health
depends on me alone, no matter
my circumstances. Take a look at a
fish: the fish could care less about
what you or I think about him. He
goes about his way.

Pete: Throughout your comments
you keep referencing to the ocean.
You are very connected to it.

Cora: Yes. I have learned much
from watching God's creation.
Everyone should connect with
nature; we are part of it. People
would be much happier.

Pete: I appreciate your confidence
and openness. Let me ask you
about beauty. You said you are
beautiful. To do that, you must
compare yourself to others,
correct? I know comparison is the
essence of envy, and that is what

got this whole oppression mess started, because people were comparing you to themselves.

Cora: You are referring to physical beauty. Beauty comes from the inside, Pete. But, since you are talking about external beauty, I will share this theory: I believe throughout nature, specially throughout the animal kingdom, either the male or the female of the species holds the beauty. Beauty can be translated into the function to attract. For example, lions. The males have these amazing manes, while females don't, so I would have to say the male lions hold more beauty. Black widows are opposite, with the female being strikingly astonishing while the male black widow is tiny and ordinary looking. Some male fish grow shiny scales during breeding season. Some male birds feature more colorful feathers than their female counterparts. For humans, females hold the title; not to say there cannot be beautiful men walking around, but in general terms, women are the clear winners.

Pete: Yes. This is cross-cultural; most cultures in the world would agree with you.

Cora: There is one last thing I want to share, if I may.

Pete: Please go ahead.

Cora: I want to say to your readers the following: you did not come to this world to obey assholes. Don't listen to their lies. You do what is true, follow your heart. If you are doing wrong, your conscience will let you know, but don't let others limit you. Love your neighbors as yourself and they will love you. If they don't love you back, let them go and find another one who will.

Pete: Thank you for your energy and boldness.

Cora: My pleasure. •

LA COLIBRI

DREAMS AND VISIONS

I first saw Colibri selling admission tickets. She is the performer that closes the show every night. As the final act, she carries certain responsibility, as no one wants the final act to be a disappointment. Her act is brief, but a mighty one. She is shot out of a cannon. Yes, that sounds really wild, and it is.

Colibri has blond hair and green eyes. She is dressed in a black jumpsuit. She is thin but muscular; I guess you must be in shape to be used as a human cannonball. As she flies the crowd cheers. She travels quite a distance to land on a giant net that absorbs her landing. As she goes, she performs acrobatics in the air, reminding me of the platform divers at the Olympic games. Quite impressive, to say the least.

When we met for the interview, I realized she was very soft spoken and calm. I was expecting someone wild or loud, but I was mistaken. As with all the previous, her faith was evident during the conversation. She is gifted with dreams that really inspired me. Here is the interview.

Pete: Nice to finally meet you. I remember you selling me the admission ticket. I had no idea you were a performer as well.

Colibri: Nice to meet you as well. We are a small group, and we all have other duties than our performances. There are a lot of things going on that need everyone to pitch in. We make a great team.

Pete: That is true. All of you are a fantastic team. I have witnessed it firsthand. All of you work well and support each other. That is what makes the Carnivale a success.

Colibri: Thank you. I love my sisters.

Pete: How did you come up with your act? It is certainly extremely dangerous. And that cannon!

Colibri: I inherited it from my predecessor. I joined the Carnivale very young, and I was her assistant for many years until she retired. She taught me all about it: how operate safely and correctly. I came to enjoy the preparations, how to set up the cannon, the explosives, the science behind it. It is actually a lot of fun, a shot of adrenaline every time. I love to fly in the air, even if it is just for an instant.

Pete: I deduct you must be very precise. No margin for error.

Colibri: That's correct. If the load is not accurate, I could land outside the net, and I would not bounce back from that. There are other factors, like the air humidity and such. It's really a science.

Pete: Well, it was amusing to witness. Thank you for doing that. As you know, I have been interviewing all the performers. They have been very kind in sharing their supernatural stories with me. I am very grateful. What would you like to share?

Colibri: Sure. I am happy to share. God has given me foresight through dreams, as well as messages of different kinds. I have a few stories to share.

Pete: Do you mean foresight as in dreams of the future?

Colibri: Yes. I have experienced those on a few of occasions.

Pete: Can you tell me about it?

Colibri: Yes. These dreams are different from regular dreams. I call them visions. The reason being is that they are not a product of my mind. I have been given visions of things to come; things I would otherwise would not know about.

Let me start by telling you about this vision I had many years ago. In the vision, I was looking at the sky. There were fireballs falling from the sky. They were like meteors of lava. All around me was fire, and I was standing on a rock, looking up. Even though there was so much destruction around me, I was safe. I was holding two little kids by their hands. We were all witnessing the event. They were my kids, even though I was unmarried and didn't have kids at the time. I woke up thinking, where was the father of my children? My husband? I was wondering why he was not with us. Why he was not part of the dream?

Pete: You were unmarried at the time, and had no kids, correct? What do you think the meaning was of that vision?

Colibri: First I thought I was witnessing the end of the world. It just didn't make sense at the time. I kept going on with my life. A decade later I got married, and gave birth to two children, a boy and a girl, just like in the dream. When they were still little, about five and six years old, the age they were in the dream, I went through a terrible divorce. My husband destroyed my life in the process: everything around me was devastated. I was completely broke, with practically no money, because he had mismanaged our finances so badly.

I lost all my friends because he lied about me to everyone, blaming me for the divorce, and making false accusations. My world went up in fire, just like in the vision. But even though that was devastating, my kids and I were ok.

Pete: The vision became true!

Colibri: I think it was God preparing me, many years in advance, for this event. This was a revelation that finally became clear sometime after the divorce. I know it was God telling me it was going to be ok, that my kids and I were going to be protected, He had His eyes on me.

Pete: Astonishing!

Colibri: Thank you. This leads me to share another sign I received pertaining the divorce. The father moved to another house and a week later he was scheduled to make a visit to pick up the kids. That was the first day my children will be separated from me since they were born. When the father arrived, a few minutes later a white dove landed on my bedroom window. The dove had a few brown feathers on her back and chest. The dove sat on the window and started staring at me. There are a few things about this sighting that makes it very unusual. That type of doves are not common in the area. When the dove landed, even the father

noticed and said: "interesting". The dove sat there for a long time, staring at me. I know it was a message from God, telling me to be courageous, that He was looking after me and the kids.

Pete: Did you ever see another dove like that again?

Colibri: Never. Like I said, there are no doves around because hawks, owls, and eagles, are prevalent in that area. They eat doves and other smaller birds.

Pete: What did you feel when you saw it, staring at you?

Colibri: Peace. The sadness of my kids leaving and the anger I had towards my ex-husband disappeared. This was much bigger than my current circumstances.

Pete: It does match the narrative. That is very reassuring, to know, that God is looking out for you.

Colibri: For all of us, Pete.

Pete: That was very interesting. Tell me about the next dream you wanted to share.

Colibri: Another vision I had was similar to the first. I saw the country being devastated on a specific date. The country was going to collapse 6 months in the future. All its finances and structure, its ability to make business, all gone. I woke up and wrote down the date. I was shaken, because it was a bad situation. However, I felt I was going to be ok; I just had to go through the experience.

Pete: So, when the date came what happened?

Colibri: I actually forgot about it. Life was going as usual, and the country was fine. Then I fell sick out of nowhere. I was incredibly sick, and I thought I was going to die. I lost all my strength and was unable to work. I saw all my efforts to build a life vanish. Nothing mattered. There was a sense of despair and wasted efforts. All I fought for was for nothing. It was only after two weeks that I started to turn the corner. I eventually recovered. When I was good enough to work, I found my note, and I cried. I got a divine warning and had forgotten about it.

Pete: Well, both dreams would have been hard to understand from the moment you had them.

Colibri: I agree, but this is proof that God is present in our lives, present, past, and future. He cares about us, with love, and knows the challenges we will face. Let's move on and allow me to tell you about the next vision.

Pete: Please do.

Colibri: The next vision is actually two separate dreams. A year before my parents passed away, which occurred five months apart, is when I received the first vision. I entered a house, that looked like a primitive shack, made of sticks and a roof of hay. When I walked in I saw three people inside, talking to each other. I locked eyes with the man in the middle. He was wearing a simple brown tunic tied up with a rope, and sandals. He had tan skin, and was of average size and build, had dark brown hair up to his shoulders, and a short beard. His eyes were brown and was average looking. Somehow I immediately knew who He was. It was Jesus! There was no doubt. I was shocked!

Pete: What!?

Colibri: I couldn't move. Like I said, I was shocked in awe. His eyes were full of kindness, love and power. I looked at Him and I heard Him speak even though His lips didn't move. I felt His power and Holiness going through my soul. He told me everything was going to be ok; to have peace. Then I woke up.

Pete: How did you know it was Jesus and not your imagination?

Colibri: The vision was real; I was in His Holy presence. I remember His

face up to this day; majestic.
I know dreams are often confusing.
This one was as real and clear as
I am speaking to you right now.
The details were all there.

Pete: Is there a difference between
a dream and a vision?

Colibri: Yes, there is. The second
dream came a week later after
the first. I was suddenly in this
field covered with wheat. There
was a hill, and I saw Jesus, walking
accompanied by others, whom
I assume were His apostles.
This time He didn't speak to me,
but I realized He was very busy.
Somehow, I got the message that
He was working because time was
running short, and the harvest
was coming. He told me he was
busy and that is why He seemed
distant, because He was focusing
on the tasks at hand, so I had to be
patient and just wait. He walked
away and I looked uphill. There was
a river coming from the top of the
hill. It was a river with living water.
The river was coming through an
entrance in a stone wall at the
top of the hill. I knew that was the
entrance to heaven. I wanted to
go up and look through the door,
so I started walking. When I was
reaching the entrance, I saw a
light, like a beautiful yellow sunset,
coming through the gate. Then
I heard the message; it was not time
for me to enter, and I woke up.

Pete: Was that a familiar place?

Colibri: I have never seen that place
before, but it was not foreign.
I know it was real. I was in there.
It reminds me of John 14: 1–3,
where Jesus mentions not to be
troubled, and that He is preparing a
place for us, so we can be with Him.
I cannot wait. There is nothing else
I desire more than that.

Pete: I admire your strong faith.
Thank you for sharing.

Colibri: Shalom •

TRUTH WILL MAKE YOU FREE